For Hattie xx
H.W.

To Finnick, *my newborn*
who was generous to share his mommy
with The Snow Princess

To *my husband,* Kyle, *and* my parents,
who always support and believe in me
H.H.

First published in 2015 by Scholastic Children's Books
Euston House, 24 Eversholt Street
London NW1 1DB
a division of Scholastic Ltd
www.scholastic.co.uk
London ~ New York ~ Toronto ~ Sydney ~ Auckland
Mexico City ~ New Delhi ~ Hong Kong

Text copyright © 2015 Holly Webb
Illustrations copyright © 2015 Helen Huang

PB ISBN 978 1407 15722 1

HOLLY WEBB

The Snow Princess

illustrated by Helen Huang

SCHOLASTIC

Once upon a time, many years ago, a tiny baby
was born in the middle of winter, when the snow
was deep and cold. She was born in a grand palace, and
she was a princess. She was the first and only child of
the king and queen, and the whole country loved her.

The baby princess grew up, just like any other baby – except that Princess Amy had rooms full of toys, and servants to do everything that she wanted. But even so, she was sweet and kind.

She loved to play in the palace gardens and feed crumbs to the birds, and they grew tame enough to take the food from her hands.

As the little princess got older, her toys and her clothes were finer and more precious with every passing year, until it came to her tenth birthday.

"This birthday is special," the queen told her daughter. "You are starting to grow up. We must have a party grander than any before."

"Must we?"
sighed Princess Amy,
gazing at the swans
sailing down the river.

For weeks and weeks after that, no one talked to the little princess about anything but parties and dresses and cake. Everything had to be perfect – the queen had said so.

"Oh, Princess Amy," whispered her best friend Bella, who was the daughter of the palace cook, "you must be so excited!"

Amy thought that Bella was much more excited than she was. If only she could spend her birthday building snowmen with Bella, wearing her oldest clothes. But although the winter was bitterly cold, no snow had fallen.

"What would you like for your birthday, Amy dear?" her ladies-in-waiting kept on asking. "Jewels? Shoes? An elephant?"

"An elephant?" Amy yelped.

"Oh, yes, an elephant!" They nodded delightedly. "How grand."

"An elephant?" Bella whispered, round-eyed.
"Won't the poor thing get cold?"

The queen frowned at her daughter. "If you don't want an elephant – and perhaps that's sensible, as I can't think where we'd put it – what do you want for your birthday, Amy dear? We have to give you something!"

Amy watched the icy river, and saw
a little boy picking up firewood under the
trees. She thought he looked hungry.
"Do you? I don't think I need anything else."

"Really, she's impossible," the queen
muttered to the ladies-in-waiting,
and they all agreed.

Everywhere that Amy went, there were people fussing about her birthday.
"Oh, Princess!" smiled the cook. "You shouldn't be down here in the kitchens."
But she let Amy and Bella cut out biscuits.

"This party, Princess," she sighed. "A seventy-three course dinner! I've
hardly slept in a week, and I keep having nightmares about trifle."

Princess Amy sighed,
and gave the cook a hug.
She didn't much like trifle either.

"I wish," the princess said to herself, on the morning before her birthday, "I wish it would snow. That would be the nicest birthday present of all."

She opened her window and peered out at the cold grey sky. Then she fetched a biscuit to feed the little birds looking at her hopefully from the windowsill.

Just then, the queen called her to hurry
and try on her new dress for the party, and
Amy didn't see the two little birds fly away,
twittering excitedly to each other.

The rest of the day was a whirl of dress fittings,

and dancing lessons and fuss.

The little princess went to bed
that night very tired. She wished
she could be as happy about her
birthday as everyone else was.

That night, the snow came, just as
the little princess had wished. The birds had flown
up into the sky with magic shining from their feathers.
They chirruped the princess' wish to the wind,
and the snow began to fall.

Amy laughed and leapt out of bed, sweeping the sugary
white snow off the ledge as she threw the window open.
"Thank you," she whispered out into the sky,
and a flurry of snowflakes swirled down to
land shimmering on her hair.

Princess Amy danced down the stairs to find the king and queen.

But her father was standing on the terrace, gazing out anxiously.

"Don't you like the snow?" the princess asked him.

"It's beautiful – but our people are cold and hungry,

out there in the town," he murmured.

The princess slipped
her hand into his
and asked, "Couldn't we
invite everyone to my party?"

As the party began, Princess Amy stepped out onto the ice, with her hand in Bella's. They were slipping and sliding and laughing, and both of them were crowned with snowflakes.

All around them, people were dancing, full of delicious food,
with lots more to take home too.

The little princess swung her best friend round and round,
and whispered, "This is just the birthday I wished for."